To N.A., my one true love and my soul's inspiration.

Thank you to my siblings, who read and critiqued whatever I sent them at the drop of a hat. A sincere thank you to Amy Novesky, my editor, who encouraged me to write this true story. You are the best.

In loving memory of my mama, Mattie E. Noel, and my sister, Melva Noel.
—M.N.

For mamas raising readers—thank you.
—D.P.

Text copyright © 2024 Melvina Noel
Illustrations copyright © 2024 Daria Peoples

Pages 2–3, 16, 30–31: Color lithograph of Sissieretta Jones, Library of Congress,
Prints and Photographs Division, Alfred Bendiner Memorial Collection, LC-DIG-var-1857

Pages 2–3, 16, 30–31: Hand-colored lithograph of historic Black men, Library of Congress,
Prints and Photographs Division, LC-DIG-pga-02252

Pages 2–3, 6, 16, 30–31: *Narrative of the life of Frederick Douglass, an American slave*,
Library of Congress, Rare Book and Special Collections Division, LOC Control # 82225385

Pages 2–3, 17, 30–31: Photograph of Sojourner Truth, Library of Congress,
Prints and Photographs Division, Gladstone Collection of African American Photographs, LC-DIG-ppmsca-08978

Pages 2–3, 16, 30–31: Cabinet card of African American cowgirl from Anaconda, Montana, ca. 1900;
UC San Diego; Steve Turner Collection of African-Americana

Pages 2–3, 16, 30–31: Photograph of Black judge,
Cut Out and Collage: Vintage African American Ephemera by Ada Ashley

Book design by Melissa Nelson Greenberg
These images were created using oil paints, watercolor, pencil, charcoal, and Photoshop.

Library of Congress Cataloging-in-Publication Data available.
ISBN: 978-1-949480-23-8

Printed in China   10 9 8 7 6 5 4 3 2 1

Cameron Kids books are available at special discounts when purchased in quantity for premiums and
promotions as well as fundraising or educational use. Special editions can also be created to specifications.
For details, contact specialsales@abramsbooks.com or the address below.

ABRAMS The Art of Books
195 Broadway, New York, NY 10007
abramsbooks.com

CHECKOUT

APRIL 15 1965			
MAY 19 1963			
AUG 28 1963			
AUG 29 1963			
JUNE 19 1964			
JULY 2 1964			
MAR 7 1965			
MAR 25 1965			

MAMA'S LIBRARY SUMMERS

BY MELVINA NOEL

ART BY DARIA PEOPLES

cameron kids

For Mama, summer vacation means reading books—lots of them!

Every summer Mama drives me and my sister to the library to check out books. Only books about Black people, Mama's directions. We read all summer long.

Mama always waits in the car. Motor on. Air conditioning running. Cool minutes. Motor off. Windows down. Flapping her hand to fan herself. Hot seconds. Windows up. Motor on.

Me and my sister know exactly where to find our books.

We plop down on the library floor. We pull books, counting each one. Ten books a person, the library's limit. We stack our chosen books on the floor between us.

"We read that one before. Mama said no repeats," my sister whispers. No repeats. Hard to choose. No repeats. Some books aren't children's books at all. We need a dictionary.

The librarian stands over us. "No more than three books on the same subject!" We look at the librarian, then at each other.

I close my eyes. Pick three. Open my eyes. Slide the rest back on the shelf. "Next time," I whisper to the books. My sister copies me.

And so it goes. Pick books. Put some books back. Pull other books out.

Grinning, we walk out of the library tightly hugging and balancing ten books apiece.

Mama opens the car door. "What took so long? Don't you know how hot it is in this car?" Mama doesn't come inside because she is too shy.

"Yes, Mama," I mumble. Me and my sister take turns reading the back cover of each book out loud to Mama while we drive home.

At home, my sister, Mama, and I scan the twenty books spread across my bed. Then we choose one. Grab a book like it's gold.

Soon I am lying on my bed, my sister on the floor, and Mama in her reading chair. The three of us disappear into our books . . .

Heart racing, I run through the woods
with Harriet Tubman. At night.
Escaping slavery. Just want to be free.

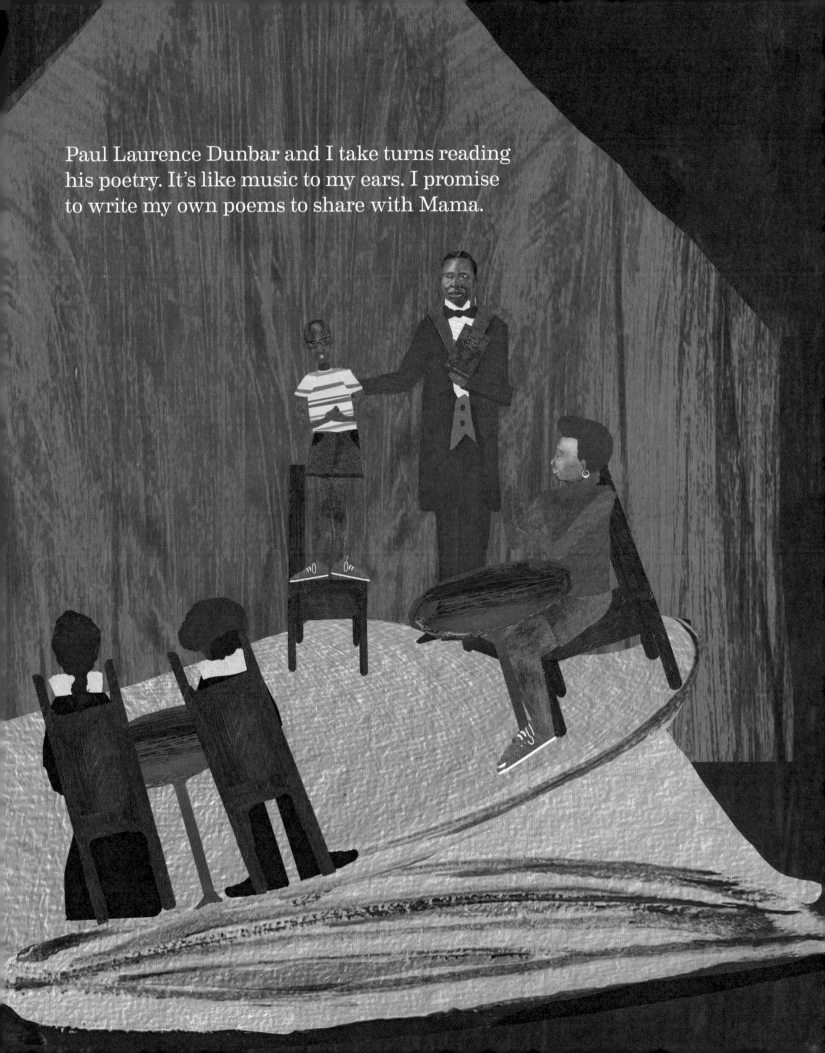

Paul Laurence Dunbar and I take turns reading his poetry. It's like music to my ears. I promise to write my own poems to share with Mama.

I stand in Washington, DC, among thousands of people.
Chanting "I have a dream" with Dr. Martin Luther King Jr.

I see myself in our library books. I learn about Africa. Slavery. Civil rights. Black contributions to America. I am proud to be Black, thanks to Mama.

When we are done with our books, Mama holds book review contests. We each share loud, strong opinions about each book. Winner gets an extra slice of Mama's homemade sweet potato pie.

The summer ends way too fast.
My sister and I return our books,
leaving the library empty-handed,
but holding hands.

Mama opens the car door, and
when she sees our sad faces, she
says, "Don't worry. Next summer
will be here before you know it."

AUTHOR'S NOTE

I absolutely love reading books. And the person responsible for that love is my mama. She filled the hole that the schools left empty for Black children. I grew up in a time when schools did not teach Black history or any of the contributions that Black people made to America. So, Mama made it her mission to make sure we read about Black people across all subjects. During the school year, my sister and I checked out a few books at a time.

The author with her mother and sister.

But during the summer, there was a wonderful explosion of reading in our house. Checking out twenty books that my sister and I got to choose was just the beginning of the magic. Books about Black people were the main attraction. We did not see ourselves in our schoolbooks, nor did we learn Black history from our teachers. But in our library books, we saw us. We saw the struggles, the strength, the love, the hope, and the happiness of Black people who never gave up on their dreams. The books we read were raising us to be the same.

And the beauty of our summer reading was that my sister and I got to do it with Mama, spending quality time together discussing and debating books. And these were not just children's books—these books covered a range of topics across many genres, like poetry, fiction, and nonfiction. Some of the books required extensive use of the dictionary. But Mama was there to guide us, teach us, and help us enjoy reading. She created wonderful, loving memories that stayed with me long after childhood—memories even sweeter than her delicious homemade sweet potato pie.

Today, I continue to read about Black people, especially books by Black authors on various topics. But my reading has also expanded to all types of books by authors of all backgrounds: poetry, science fiction, romance, self-help, children's books, spiritual . . . well, you get the picture. And thanks to reading so many books with Mama during short periods of time, I now typically read a minimum of three books of different genres at the same time. It is like traveling to different countries in one trip. There is no shortage of fun, excitement, and discovery.

And my home—it looks like a library, with lots of books in every room. Thanks, Mama!

ILLUSTRATOR'S NOTE

When I was a little girl, I loved to ride my bike, draw pictures, and play basketball. I loved all sports that involved catching and throwing. I was a really good thrower. But if I'm being truthful, there was one activity I did not like very much. If you can believe it, it was reading—and I kept this a secret from my parents for as long as possible because they were both teachers!

But when my mom figured out that I didn't like to read, she took matters into her own hands. Just like the mama in *Mama's Library Summers*, my mama took me to the library. She told the librarian I needed a job! At nine years old, I worked as a page in our town's public library. To my surprise, while I helped the librarian, she helped me find books I enjoyed, which I'm certain was all part of my mother's plan. My hometown library inspired a lot of the art in *Mama's Library Summers*.

The illustrator with her mother.

All the mamas in my family influenced me to become a reader and a storyteller. My mother always made sure my brothers and I had several books to choose from in our home at all times. Her mother, Nana, was an avid reader and introduced my mom to the love of reading, and Nana's mother and my great-grandmother, Granma, read and wrote poetry. I also vividly remember watching Momo, my father's mother, reading the newspaper and her Bible every day in her recliner. The ideas for the decor inside the house in *Mama's Library Summers* came from Momo's home.

Reading wasn't my first love, but through my many visits to the library, I discovered engaging stories I loved to read. Today, my house is filled with many, many interesting books that inspire me to write and illustrate stories. I'm very grateful my mama took me to the library.